High Heat

Naughty Brutal Aroused Scorching Hottest Explicit

Romantic Stories

Lana Kendra

This is a work of fiction; names, characters, places, and incidents are either the product of the author's imagination or are used fictitiously, and any resemblance to actual people, living or dead, business establishments, events, or locales is entirely coincidental.

This e-book is for your personal use only and may not be resold or given to anyone else. If you want to give this book to someone else, please buy an extra copy for each person. If you're reading this book and didn't buy it, or if it wasn't bought for your personal use only, go back to your favorite ebook retailer and buy your copy. Thank you for acknowledging this author's efforts.

Table of Contents

Content Warning

Due to its sexual content, this book is only for those over the age of legal adulthood. There are some topics with a lot of foul language. All of the characters are at least eighteen years old.

Introduction

Are you in search of an exciting and thrilling book to read? Look no further than this extensive collection of Erotic Suspense book. I offer a wide range of genres, including Romantic Erotica, Fantasy, and Urban BDSM Fiction, to cater to even the most discerning reader. Whether you enjoy Anthologies, Westerns, or Paranormal Romance, I have something to suit your taste. My collection also includes Poetic Folklore, Interracial, Black & African American Literary Criticism, and Gothic Horror for those who crave a deeper and darker reading experience. If you're interested in Futuristic, LGBTQ+, Short Stories, or Lesbian literature, my diverse range of options will keep you captivated. Additionally, I offer Humorous, Victorian, New Adult, and College Women's Psychological Mysteries for those seeking a lighter but equally engaging read. Furthermore, My Fairy Tale Collections,

Transgender, Contemporary Western, Bisexual, and Poetry genres will transport you to different worlds and explore a variety of themes. For my Teen and Young Adult readers, I have a selection of European Geography, Cultures, eBooks, Loners, Outcasts, Mythology, Folk Tales, and much more. With such a wide array of options to choose from, you'll never run out of thrilling and enchanting stories to immerse yourself in.

It is important to emphasize that this content is exclusively intended for individuals who are 18 years of age or older.

High Heat

Everybody's life was severely disrupted by the pandemic, both those who suffered and those who had to care for or live with those who did. But single women like me also lost everything during the shutdown.

My sexual life was completely destroyed by being unable to move around. I played with my toys throughout the start of the lockdown, which temporarily eased my anxiety, but I soon missed the sensation of being a real guy. I missed the amazing sensation of the dick's first penetration into my pussy and the power of his arms as he twisted and turned me around. I missed putting my legs over his back and experiencing the ecstasy that tore through my body as his dick pushed beyond my uterus and into the depths of my pussy.

When the lockdown was lifted, I was literally going insane.

For the first week or two, I was really busy working on the project, but after it was done, I wanted to celebrate. I required a good fuck.

In order to celebrate finishing the assignment successfully, I called my favorite dick, a massive 10-inch black dick. I was granted some time off from work. When I heard his voice, I got really delighted. I lost it on him when he told me he was ordered up north to solve a problem, even though we were both needing one other. After all, I realized it wasn't his fault, so I apologized. That night, I slept with my 10-inch dildo in my ass and Rabbit in my pussy. I came so often that I exhausted myself. After dragging myself to the restroom, I soaked for more than an hour before turning in.

I was just as horny when I woke up the following day. I needed to get fucked because the pranks from the previous night had no effect. I made the decision to go out for breakfast in an attempt to distract myself from my condition because I didn't have a backup plan. I made the decision to don a short dress so I could flaunt the toned legs I gained over the pandemic.

When I arrived at the restaurant, I had to wait to be seated. The personnel appeared to be active, and there were a fair number of individuals present. One of the staff members was counting the number of customers when I noticed him peering into the kitchen. Before I sat down, I gave him a quick once over and thought he looked good.

I wanted to wash my hands once I was seated, so I asked to use the restrooms. On my way there, I had to pass by the kitchen and storerooms, and the young man I had seen earlier emerged from the storeroom as I turned the corner. We had to smile at each other when we brushed past one other because the passageway was so small. I went on to wash my hands in the restrooms. I had hardly emerged from the restroom when he turned the corner once more and headed in the other direction. He pressed me against the wall and put his hands between my legs as we were about to brush past each other. He had amazing aim. He located my clit and gave it a good flick before sticking two fingers inside my pussy. I clutched his shoulder and started to fuck his finger; it felt fantastic, like the first male contact I've had in months. As my pussy gushed, I asked him to extend his finger. But rather than sticking another finger in my pussy, he escorted me back into the bathroom. In my lustful mood, I knew just what to do. I leaned over, lifted my skirt, and entered a cubicle. The young man, aware that we didn't have much time, jumped into my pussy and gave me a wild, passionate fuck. He was giving me what I wanted, a real dick, and his dick was a decent size. We gathered together, me squealing and bucking beside him, moaning and grunting.

After we cleaned up, I gave him a cheek kiss to express

my gratitude. I made my way back upstairs to my table and ate my breakfast to the fullest. Even though it was a hot fuck, it did not much lessen the pain. I required extra.

I made the decision to go shopping after breakfast, but I wanted to try somewhere different. For a change of scenery, I drove 40 miles to a sizable shopping center.

The mall was bustling with people from all social classes when I entered. I was walking around the mall, still high from my breakfast fuck, and I could feel the energy of men and women smiling at me. I was strolling through the mall idly when I spotted a Victoria Secret. I made the decision to walk inside and check if I could add any new toys to my already enormous collection. A number of couples were perusing lingerie sets, while numerous young women were admiring attractive undergarments. Conversely, I headed right toward the toy department.

There weren't many people down there, and it was

peaceful. The sales assistant approached me as I was perusing the directions on a remote-controlled sex toy and admiring the assortment of dildos.

Do you need assistance?"She asked in a professional manner, looking shocked by my answer at first, but then beaming broadly.

I responded with a pretty devilish smirk on my lips, "That depends on what you had in mind."

She told me who she was, Lana, and started gushing over the quality of the remote-controlled toy. I asked, "You seem to know this product very well. Have you used one?" while she was demonstrating how to use it. She leaned forward and lifted her short plaid skirt at that point. The toy's pale blue end was peeking out of her bare pussy.

I exclaimed, "Wow, your pussy looks beautiful with the toy peeping out," as a massive rush of adrenaline shot through my body. She handed me the remote and instructed me to turn it up, so I did. She started to moan and move her hips. I clicked the remote again, and she let out a yelp as the intensity went up further. She turned around and pulled me close, kissing me deeply as her orgasm hit. I held her close and was grinding my pussy on to her when she reached between my legs and began to play with my clit. Her touch was so soft and tender that I started to fuck her fingers much like I did earlier. I came so quickly that it caught me off guard, and I unintentionally clicked the remote again.

With a wide smile on my face, I left the store and strolled through the mall. By the time I got to the car in the late afternoon, I was thinking to myself, "We're having fun today," as I smiled.

I went to sleep satisfied with my many orgasms but still needed to feel a guy inside of me after spending that night playing with my new toy until I almost passed out.

The next morning, my phone rang and it was one of my northern girlfriends, inviting me to her sister's birthday party tomorrow night. I was going to have to make the trip because Sandra and I were friends in secondary school and we used to get into a lot of trouble together, plus it would be a change of pace and an opportunity to catch up on her life.

The only other person in the carriage was a well-dressed man who was about 6 feet tall, and although he had no obvious special qualities, there was something about him that was holding my attention. Maybe I was wearing my "horny" glass while I was examining him. About 15 minutes into the journey, he gets up and comes up to me and introduces himself. I boarded the train, found a quiet section in first class, bought a gin and tonic, and settled down with my music for the lengthy ride.

We talked for a while, getting to know each other a little as the time passed; from the tent rising in his pants, I would say he was being turned on; to be honest, I was getting wet from the conversation as well; from the size of the tent, I would say he had a nice dick. I was still very horny and being alone with this man gave me an idea. "Hello, I'm Adrian and I have been watching you from the time we left the station." I introduced myself and he asked if he could join me.

I told Adrian I had to use the restroom, spreading my legs a little to show him my nude pussy and then doing my best walk to express my desires. Just as I was about to enter the restroom, I noticed Adrian had started to follow me. He locked the bathroom door behind him and gave me a passionate embrace, grabbing my breasts as I tried to free his dick, which he assisted me in getting free, and as soon as it was, I sat down and he started to suck my dripping pussy. I couldn't wait any longer, so I got up and leaned over to feel Adrian's sexy and powerful.

I was enjoying the sex, but to my dismay, Adrian came too soon for me to cum. He came growling, and when his sperm hit my mouth, I began to suck him hard. His dick was shooting sperm into my mouth, but the rest of him was stiff. I released his dick and he collapsed on to the toilet. I cleaned my pussy, feeling a bit unfulfilled, and left him in there to recover. When he finally emerged from the restroom, I had bought him a drink from the attendant and was enjoying some downtime.

I went to bed reliving the week I had so far: I got fucked in a restaurant on Tuesday morning, had a woman play with my pussy on Tuesday afternoon, played with my new toy until I almost passed out on Thursday, and got fucked on a train on Friday. All in all, my week was going well and without my favorite dick. Sandra picked me up from the station, and we spent the rest of the evening chatting and catching up on each other's lives.

When we got to the location, we were seated at tables, kind of like at a wedding reception, with the intention of having a good time and playing games before sending the kids and their parents home so the real fun could start.

After introducing me to the two men and two women who were already seated at the singles table, Sandra led me over and we struck up a light discussion to pass the time.

Wearing a blue lace lingerie set that made me feel quite seductive, and with a man seated on either side of me, my clothing accentuated my form in a slightly conservative way, keeping in mind that there would be older people and children present.

The games began and everyone was having a great time when I felt a hand on the inside of my thigh. Joseph, who was sitting to my right was getting turned on and decided to take action. He was drawing small circles about halfway up my thigh that was sending electric shocks straight to my pussy. It felt so good that I began to squirm in the seat and slide my pussy closer to his hand. My squirming must have alerted Oliver on the other side because he too was caressing my inner thigh. The pleasure from these hands made me feel delirious. Trying to keep calm and while these two men turned me on was becoming a battle too much to bear. Both hands were moving closer to my pussy, and I was becoming more and more turned on. It then occurred to me that I can't let them know the other was playing with me. Joseph got to my pussy first and immediately found my clit. I bit my lip and struggled to maintain my composure as my orgasm built rapidly. I reached down and held Oliver's hand to stop him from going any higher until I came on Joe's hand. My orgasm rippled through my body, bringing tears to my eyes as I fought to keep it under wraps. When that one subsided, I gently pushed Joe's hand down and released Oliver's hand so that he could proceed to the promised land. Oliver was even more skilled than Joe was. He found my clit and slipped a finger into my pussy to finger fuck me as well. The next orgasm came on with a full head of steam, hitting me hard. My pussy convulsed on Oliver's finger and my legs began to shake. I squeezed his hand to get him to stop which gave me the time to calm down and recover.

Oliver moved his hand, so I released Joe's and he went straight back up my thigh, soaking my panty as I squirted a few times on both hands. Having primed my pussy, he found my clit again and I came in seconds, having to pretend to sneeze to cover my scream.

I got up from the table and carefully made my way to the bathroom, where I was leaning over the sink to recuperate when Sandra entered.

With a broad smile, she remarked, "I see you have met Joe

and Oliver and have become really acquainted."

"Oh Sandra, my gosh. They had me coughing so badly that I had to wake up to avoid fainting."

Sandra exclaimed excitedly, "Well, you'll be pleased to hear that they are our dates for the evening."

Indeed, ma'am. It's going to be a great night tonight, I declared, feeling reenergized and ready for the task.

The adult party was in full swing. Sandra was grinding her pussy onto Joe's leg, while Oliver was behind and had two handfuls of breasts, and I had reached behind me and had a handful of dick. Through his jeans, his dick felt impressive, with a nice girth to it. I paired up with Oliver, but I had a sneaking suspicion that I was going to fuck both tonight. The four of us were dancing like we were the only people there.

When the pressure got to me, I said to Sandra, "We need

to go, I need some dick." She said she was fine, told the boys we were ready, and the four of us bid the party farewell and headed out when Joe announced they had rented a room nearby so they could make the most of their time. We all laughed at his considerateness.

I looked over at Sandra just before I came; she had her legs in the air and was squealing because Joe was eating her pussy. The hotel was five minutes walk away. Oliver pushed me up against the wall and his hand was between my legs in a flash. He found my clit and was massaging it while he kissed me deeply.

I yelled loudly, declaring that I would not be hiding or holding back, and my orgasm shook my whole body, causing me to squirt all over Oliver's shirt.

"Very nice," he grinned, dropping to his knees and starting to nibble my pussy. My whining and swearing were drowned out by Sandra's cumming, which shook her like an earthquake and left her with Joe's head locked in place with her hands and legs. I'm not sure how well Joe was breathing, but he sure as hell rode that wave of ecstasy.

After deciding to follow my lead and strip off, I moved away from Oliver and laid down on the bed next to Sandra. It was then that I saw the two dicks we were going to play with tonight: Joe's was about the same length but thinner than Oliver's, measuring about 8 to 9 inches.

Oliver approached me with the intention of eating my pussy, but I was already hot and wanted to fuck, so I shot him a straight "fuck me" look and he got up, smiling, and shoved his dick between my pussy lips.

"Oh my god, stop teasing me" was my desperate cry as he positioned his dick at the entrance and moved slowly into my pussy. I have always cherished the sensation of the first stroke, stretching my pussy, and Oliver did just that, pushing his dick balls deep and then slowly pulling them back out to the tip. He then repositioned me on the bed and started to fuck me hard, each stroke full length and powerful. Having been turned on from the party, it didn't take long for my first orgasm to occur.

Joe had Sandra in the same position as me, screaming, and soon after I felt like I was about to cum, I grabbed his arms, threw my head back, and let out a guttural cry, "ARGGGGGHHHHH, FUCK," as this orgasm tore through my body. The two young men were fucking us so good that we were both screaming and grunting as we came again.

Sandra was still on his back, letting Joe pound the hell out of her; she was swearing and slapping him every time she came, which seemed to turn him on even more. I pushed Oliver off me and told him to lay on his back. I had to take control or I would pass out from the way this man was fucking me. Straddling his body, I stroked his glistening dick a couple of times before putting into my pussy and sitting all the way down on it.

I sat all the way down on Oliver's dick, moaned as his dick head flicked past my internals and tapped my G-spot, and then I repositioned to get his dick right where I wanted it before I started to fuck him. After I was comfortable, I started to ride him hard, my pussy gushing, and he told me that he could feel my hot pussy juice running down his balls. That comment turned me on so much that I lifted my hips, slammed my pussy back down on his dick, and came with such force, that I squirted onto his belly.

I was just starting to calm down from my orgasm when Sandra came back. Joe was in excellent shape and was still pounding her pussy. She seemed to be having a stronger orgasm than before because she was thrashing and shaking, so I pushed Joe off her and rolled to the side of the bed shaking. I was still riding Oliver when Joe grabbed my hips. I felt his dick at the entrance to my ass and I froze. He applied a little pressure and the head popped in. I threw my head back with my mouth open, but nothing came out. Joe continued to push and his dick got even deeper.

"God, please!"I cried out as he pushed his ass even further up my ass and I felt his balls hit my ass cheeks. He began to fuck me slowly, letting my ass get used to his dick and then as it loosened up, he fucked me faster and harder. Oliver was matching Joe's strokes and I was riding a wave of euphoria being full of dick. When Oliver grabbed my breasts and started to suck both nipples simultaneously, I lost my composure and slammed my hips up and down on both dicks. Later, I was told that I was punching Oliver while I was cumming. The guys released me and I rolled onto the floor still shaking.

It must have been only a few minutes after I passed out because when I woke up, the guys had Sandra in a similar sandwich with Oliver in her ass; she was having the time of her life, and I went over to give her some support, and she grabbed my arm, opening her mouth as though to say something, but it was a massive orgasm.

I'm cumming, fuck, fuck, fuck!" and she began to shake like she had just been tased. Now I have known Sandra for many years and I know when she cums, her pussy convulses hard and she usually makes the man cum. This time was different only because she made two men cum. Joe was the to cum grunting and groaning. Oliver followed shortly, cumming deep in her ass. Both guys spoke of how hard her pussy spasmed when she came and it seemed to be magnified in her ass. I reached over to Sandra and whispered in her ear, "Thank you".

Sandra answered, "Anything for my girl," and gave me a tender kiss.

I stayed silent and watched them fuck like lovers until they finished, at which point I learned that they were indeed in love and had planned for Joe to come along for me. I was startled out of a deep slumber by the sounds of a lady groaning. Joe was still asleep.

Following breakfast, Sandra drove me back to her house so I could get my belongings before she drove me to the train station, where we said our goodbyes, exchanged kisses, and I boarded the train.

A message from Mr. 10inch arrived when I was enjoying a drink and listening to an audio book. It began, "Hey beautiful, I am back home and my front door is open." I'm wrapping up dinner and the wine is chilled. See you shortly."

"I guess I'm not going home," I grinned.

Acknowledgments

The Glory of this book's success goes to God Almighty and my beautiful Family, Fans, Readers & well-wishers, Customers, and Friends for their endless support and encouragement.

About The Author

I've spent nearly a decade penning romantic novels. As a passionate writer of erotica, I craft dark, romantic erotica. Anime Naked Truth Se of Sacred Sexuality: Forbidden Seducing Short Stories of an Erotica Nude Sexy Girl Poster. Alongside Erotic Mystery Fiction, Victorian Erotica Sex, Black & African American Erotica, Euthanasia, Daddy Teaching, Forced Domination, Alpha Monster Cuckold, and BDSM for Adults, there's an Erotic Fiction in Kinky Family. I write dark, sensual romance because I adore the power of darkness and everything that it entails. Romance novels have always been my favorite kind of books, and now I'm writing them. The idea that you will like reading and enjoying my fiction as much as I enjoy pushing the frontiers of sexual pleasure in my writing thrills me more than anything else.